Natalie
the Christmas
Stocking
Fairy

Special thanks to Rachel Elliot

ISBN 978-0-545-60540-3

12 11 10 9 8 7 6 5 4 3 2 1   14 15 16 17 18 19/0

Printed in the U.S.A.   40

First printing, September 2014

Natalie
the Christmas
Stocking Fairy

by Daisy Meadows

SCHOLASTIC INC.

The Fairyland
Palace

Living
Room

Holiday Cottage

Fairyland Christmas
Workshop

Jack Frost's
Ice Castle

Kirsty's & Rachel's
Room

Kitchen

Road to
Ice Castle

I'm fed up with Christmas and tinsel galore.
This sweet festive fuss is a drag and a bore.
The fairies have fooled me and made me look bad.
But this year I'll make them feel silly and sad!

This Christmas no stockings will fill up with toys.
No cookies or candy for good girls and boys.
I have a plan that will take all hopes away
And leave stockings empty this dark Christmas Day.

**Find the hidden letters in the stars
throughout this book. Unscramble all 8 letters
to spell a special Christmas word!**

The Magic Christmas Pie

Contents

Butter and Bother

"I love making pies at Christmastime," said Rachel Walker, sifting flour and salt into a heavy mixing bowl.

"Me, too," said her best friend, Kirsty Tate, opening a jar of cinnamon and taking a deep sniff. "The ingredients have such a Christmassy, spicy smell!"

She put the lid back on the jar and the

girls smiled happily at each other. It was the day before Christmas Eve, and they were staying in a cozy holiday cottage in the country with their families.

"Woof!" said Rachel's dog.

"You're looking forward to Christmas, too, aren't you, Buttons?" said Kirsty, leaning down to pet his shaggy head.

"What does the recipe say next?" asked Rachel, as Kirsty washed her hands.

Kirsty turned the page of the cookbook that was propped up on the kitchen counter.

"Rub the butter in with your fingers until the mixture looks like fine crumbs," she read.

Rachel opened the fridge and then frowned.

"Kirsty, did you already take the butter out of the fridge?"

"No," said Kirsty in surprise.

"That's funny," said Rachel. "I was sure we had some."

"Maybe we put it somewhere else," Kirsty suggested. "Let's look around."

They searched high and low, but the butter was nowhere to be found.

"We'll just have to go to the store again," said Rachel.

"But we're miles from anywhere," Kirsty said with a groan. "And it's almost closing time."

Just then, Mr. Tate walked into the kitchen, looking puzzled.

"Hello, girls," he said. "I just found this carton of butter on Buttons's bed. Don't you need this to make the pies?"

"Yes!" exclaimed Kirsty, giving him a delighted hug. "Thanks, Dad!"

"Greedy dog," said Mr. Tate with a chuckle, patting Buttons's head as he left the kitchen.

"That's odd," said Rachel, looking down at Buttons. "He doesn't even like butter."

Rachel rubbed the butter into the flour and then added a little water. Soon she had a ball of golden dough. She wrapped it in plastic wrap and put it in the fridge to chill.

"Should we add the secret ingredient to the pie filling now?" Kirsty suggested.

Rachel nodded eagerly.

"It's an old family secret," she said with a smile. "Our own kind of magic!"

The girls giggled happily. They knew more than most people about magic. They were secretly friends with the fairies and had had many adventures in Fairyland.

Kirsty picked up the jar of cinnamon and tried to unscrew the lid.

"Oh!" she said in surprise. "It's stuck! I must have tightened it too much when I put it back on earlier."

Rachel tried to open the jar, but it wouldn't budge.

"Let's ask my dad," she said. "He's really strong."

They hurried to the living room. Their parents were playing cards and listening to carols on the radio.

"Dad, can you undo this?" asked Rachel, holding out the spice jar. "We think Kirsty tightened it too much earlier."

Mr. Walker had to use all his strength

to open the jar. At last,
it popped open and he
handed it back to
Rachel.

"You must be
stronger than you
look, Kirsty!" he said
with a laugh.

The girls hurried back to the kitchen,
eager to add the secret ingredient. But
when they reached the doorway, they
stopped in amazement.

"What happened?" Kirsty cried.

All the drawers and cupboards were
open and there was flour all over the
kitchen. The dough was sitting on the
kitchen counter, and it was covered in
dirty fingerprints!

Suddenly, Rachel saw the top of a green head poking up from behind the kitchen counter.

"Look!" she exclaimed. "It's a goblin!"

Kirsty gasped. "What is he doing here?"

The Christmas Workshop

The goblin squawked in alarm. He flung open the back door and rushed out into the snow.

"Woof!" said Buttons, racing after him.

"Come on!" shouted Kirsty.

The girls followed Buttons out the back door, just in time to see his tail disappearing around the side of the cottage. When they reached the front yard, they found Buttons standing by the gate, barking loudly.

"Look, Kirsty," said Rachel. "Goblin footprints!"

A trail of long-toed footprints led out of the yard and into the bushes across the street.

"I wonder what a goblin is doing here the day before Christmas Eve," said Kirsty.

"I'm sure he's up to no good," said Rachel. "Maybe Jack Frost sent him. What should we do?"

"I think we have to go to Fairyland right now," said Kirsty in a determined voice. "Jack Frost and his goblins have tried to ruin Christmas before. If they're planning something again, we should tell the Christmas Fairies about it."

Rachel nodded in agreement, and the girls ran back into the cottage. Buttons was barking at their heels. He knew that something was wrong.

"Shh, Buttons," said Rachel. "It's all right. Go lie down."

As Buttons flopped down on his bed, Rachel and Kirsty hurried upstairs to the little room they were sharing. They closed the door and then opened their lockets. The lockets were presents from the queen of Fairyland, and were filled with fairy dust.

"This will take us straight to Fairyland," said Kirsty. "Then we have to find the Christmas Fairies as quickly as we can. I'm sure Jack Frost is up to something!"

They each took a pinch of fairy dust

and sprinkled it over
their heads. Instantly,
the sparkles
whirled around
them, sweeping
them off their
feet. They felt
themselves
shrinking inside
the cloud of fairy
dust.

"We're on our way to Fairyland!"
cried Kirsty in excitement.

Soon the girls were flying above one of
the magical Fairyland forests. As they
landed among the snow-topped fir trees,
they saw Crystal the Snow Fairy flying
toward them.

"Hello!" she exclaimed with a

beaming smile. "It's wonderful to see you. What brings you to Fairyland?"

Rachel quickly tried to explain. "We saw a goblin sneaking around our cottage," she said. "We think that Jack Frost might be trying to ruin Christmas again."

"We need to warn all the Christmas Fairies!" Kirsty added breathlessly.

"This is serious," said Crystal, looking worried. "I'll take you to them."

She led the way through the forest until they reached a clearing. A little wooden door was set into a grassy bank, and it was standing open as if it were waiting for them.

"This is the Christmas Workshop," said Crystal. "You'll find the Christmas Fairies inside. Good luck!"

"Thank you!" said Rachel and Kirsty together.

Crystal fluttered away, and the girls

stepped through the door.

The low workshop ceiling was twinkling with little lights that looked like stars. The smell of berries and spices filled the air. A fire was crackling in the hearth, and a snug armchair was placed close to the fireplace. Above the mantel was a large mirror, which was topped with a sprig of holly. Several stockings were hanging, and a beautiful Christmas

tree stood in the corner, dotted with tiny
flickering candles. Colorful balloons
hung above everything.

"It's beautiful," whispered Kirsty,
gazing around.

"Rachel! Kirsty!" exclaimed a tinkling
voice behind them. "Oh, thank goodness
you're here!"

The Magical Mirror

"It's Cheryl the Christmas Tree Fairy," said Rachel happily.

Cheryl fluttered toward them, holding out her hand. Behind her, they could see Holly the Christmas Fairy, Stella the Star Fairy, and Paige the Christmas Play Fairy. They were

standing around a large table beside a
tearful fairy. She had long blonde hair
and was wearing a shimmering golden
dress with orange tulle underneath. Her
gold necklace gleamed in the candlelight.

"Is something wrong?" asked Kirsty,
hugging Cheryl.

Cheryl looked across at the pretty
fairy. The table was covered with torn

paper chains and badly wrapped presents. No one looked very happy.

"Let me introduce you," she said, leading them over to the long table. "This is Natalie the Christmas Stocking Fairy."

Natalie smiled at them through her tears.

"It's wonderful to meet you," she said. "I've heard so much about you."

Rachel put her arm around the little fairy's shoulders.

"What's wrong?" she asked.

"This is where we prepare for Christmas," Natalie said. "Usually it's a really happy time. We sing carols, wrap gifts, and make decorations. But this year is different. The decorations keep breaking, the wrapping paper tears—we've even lost our box of ribbons. Everything has been going wrong!"

"Can we do anything to help?" asked Kirsty.

Natalie picked up a little box from the table. It was white, with a gold clasp and a green holly wreath carved on the top.

"This is the box where I keep my three magic items," she said. "Every year, I open it just before Christmas. My magic makes sure all the holiday preparations go well!"

She opened the box, and it started to

play "Jingle Bells."
As the music
tinkled around
the workshop,
Kirsty and
Rachel
peered into the
box.

"It's empty,"
said Kirsty in surprise.

"Yes," Natalie replied. "When
I opened the box this morning, my magic
items were gone."

She waved her wand
toward the mirror
above the
mantelpiece.
Tiny silver

snowflakes flew from her wand and scattered over the glassy surface of the mirror. When they faded, the mirror showed Jack Frost standing in the middle of the workshop. He was carrying a large sack on his back.

Rachel cried out in alarm and turned around, looking for him. Natalie shook her head.

"This is a magical mirror," she said. "It's showing us what happened here last night. Jack Frost broke in while we were all asleep."

The girls watched in horror as Jack Frost tiptoed around the workshop. When he saw Natalie's little white box, a horrible grin spread over his face. He lowered the sack to the floor.

"Ha!" he whispered, rubbing his bony hands together. "What do we have here?"

He opened the box, and the tinkling sound of "Jingle Bells" filled the air. Jack Frost looked inside, laughed, and then shook the contents of the box into his

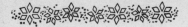

sack. He threw the box back onto the table.

"This will stop their fun once and for all," he muttered. "I've never had a visit from Santa, so why should anyone else have one?"

He scurried out of the workshop and the picture faded. Kirsty and Rachel exchanged a worried glance.

"We thought he must be up to something," said Kirsty. "We saw a goblin this morning!"

She quickly described seeing the goblin at the holiday cottage, and the other fairies looked alarmed.

"Jack Frost could have hidden Natalie's magic items anywhere," said Paige. "Where could they be—and how are we going to find them before Christmas Day?"

On the Road to the Ice Castle

"We should tell the king and queen," said Stella. "Maybe they can use their magic to see where Jack Frost has hidden Natalie's items."

"That will take too long," said Natalie. "I have to start looking now. There's not a moment to lose!"

"I have an idea," said Rachel. "Kirsty and I will stay here with Natalie and start searching. That way, the rest of you can go and tell the king and queen what's happened, and we won't waste any time."

Natalie turned to her with sparkling eyes.

"Would you really do that for me?" she asked.

"Of course," said Kirsty with a smile. "True friends always help each other out."

"It's a good idea," said Paige.

"We'll go to the palace right now," Holly added. "Good luck!"

The Christmas Fairies waved good-bye and fluttered out of the workshop.

"Now we have to decide where to start looking for the magic items," said Rachel.

"What *are* the magic items?" Kirsty asked.

"The enchanted stocking makes sure that all stockings are ready for Christmas Eve," said Natalie. "The magic Christmas pie makes sure that all Christmas treats are delicious, and the charmed candy cane makes sure that stocking gifts are perfect. But without them, no one will have a wonderful

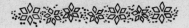

Christmas in the human or the fairy world."

"That must be why we had so much trouble making the pies," Kirsty exclaimed.

"If you were Jack Frost, where would you hide the magic items?" asked Rachel.

The girls thought carefully.

"I think we should go to the Ice Castle," said Kirsty. "If we can sneak inside, we might be able to find out where Jack Frost has hidden the things he took, even if they're not actually in the castle."

"Do you really think we should?" asked Natalie. "It could be dangerous. If Jack Frost finds us, he might imprison us."

"We've been there before and escaped,"
said Kirsty bravely. "Besides, we're not
going to let Jack Frost ruin Christmas for
everyone!"

"Kirsty's right," said Rachel. "We'll be
safe as long as we stick together."

Once out of the workshop, they
weaved their way through the trees to
the edge of the forest. At last, they found
themselves on the road to the Ice Castle.

They flew as fast as they could, keeping their eyes on the glittering castle in the distance. They were going along so quickly that they almost flew into two goblins who were arguing in the middle of the road.

"Look out!" cried Kirsty just in time.

They zipped sideways and hid behind a clump of grass at the edge of the road, panting.

"That was close!" whispered Rachel.

"Girls," said Natalie in a low voice. "Look at what that goblin has in his hand!"

The girls peeked through the thick fronds of grass to see the smaller goblin hold up a tiny, delicious-looking pie and sniff it.

"That's the magic Christmas pie!" said Natalie. "I'd recognize it anywhere!"

The goblins were arguing about what was inside the golden pastry.

"It's obviously nettle jam," the small goblin was saying. "That's why it smells so tangy."

"Don't be silly, it's minced seaweed!" the second one snapped.

"I can smell the nettles!" shouted the first.

"Well, I can smell the sea!" squawked the second.

"Nettles!"

"Seaweed!"

"Nettles!"

"Seaweed!"

"Nettles!"

Suddenly, Natalie flew out from behind the grass and hovered in front of the goblins.

"Stop!" she exclaimed.

Finders Keepers

"That's my magic Christmas pie," said Natalie. "Please give it back to me right now!"

The small goblin stuck out his tongue.

"Go away, you pesky fairy," he said. "This is mine."

Kirsty and Rachel flew out to join Natalie.

"It's not yours," said Kirsty. "You shouldn't take things that don't belong to you."

"We found it in the Ice Castle," said  the small goblin. "Finders keepers, losers weepers," added the other goblin. "We're going to make a whole tray of Christmas pies for Jack Frost."

Suddenly, Rachel noticed that the end of the small goblin's nose was speckled with flour.

"You were in our holiday cottage today, weren't you?" she exclaimed. "What were you doing there?"

The little goblin looked
embarrassed. He scuffed
his long green toes on
the dusty road.

"We just wanted to
learn how to make pies,"
he said. "But you came
back before I could find
out what was inside."

"That's easy," said
Kirsty. "We were making
my grandmother's special recipe."

"What's in that?" demanded the bigger
goblin.

"It has apples and brown sugar," said
Kirsty.

"And lemon zest and pecans," Rachel
added.

The goblins made faces. The small

goblin wrinkled his nose in disgust.

"Yuck!" he said. "Horrible sickly sweet fairy food."

"What a rotten trick," grumbled the other. "I'm glad we didn't try the pie!"

Suddenly, Kirsty had an idea. She turned to Natalie and Rachel with shining eyes.

"I think I know how to get the magic Christmas pie back," she said. "Natalie, could you use your magic to make a special batch of pies? They would have to be filled with something the goblins would really like."

"Yes, of course," said Natalie. "But why?"

Kirsty smiled at her and turned to the goblins.

"Goblins, how would you like to have a delicious hot batch of nettle and seaweed pies?" she asked.

Their eyes grew big and the small one licked his lips hungrily.

"Natalie could make you as many pies as you can carry," Kirsty continued.

"Yes!" squawked the goblins. "Give us the nettle pies!"

"All you have to do is give us that Christmas pie you're holding," said Kirsty.

The small one thrust the magic pie into Natalie's hands. It immediately returned to fairy-size, and Rachel sighed in relief.

Then Natalie waved her wand, and a huge tray of steaming-hot pies appeared in front of the goblins. Green ribbons of steam wafted under the girls' noses.

Rachel and Kirsty thought the new pies smelled very strange, but the goblins

were delighted.
They each
grabbed
several pies
and gobbled
them down
greedily.

"Wonderful!" they cried, spraying crumbs everywhere. "Delicious!"

They rushed off toward the Ice Castle, holding the large tray of pies between them. Natalie turned to the girls with a big smile.

"We did it!" said Rachel, clapping her hands in delight.

"You have helped me so much," Natalie said. "How can I ever thank you?"

"We're happy to help," said Kirsty. "We don't want Jack Frost to ruin Christmas morning!"

"Thank you," said Natalie. "I have to return the magic Christmas pie to its box now, but will you help me look for the enchanted stocking and the charmed candy cane?"

"Definitely!" said Rachel, hugging their new friend. "We'll be at our cottage when you need us."

Natalie waved her wand at the girls' lockets. They filled up with fairy dust again, and closed all by themselves.

"I'll see you soon," she said. "And 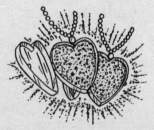 thank you again. I couldn't have done it without you!"

With another wave of

Natalie's wand, the girls were showered
with silvery
fairy dust,
which swirled
around them.
They held hands
as the magic
lifted them off
their feet to start
the journey home. They
couldn't wait for their next
adventure with Natalie—
but right now they had some
Christmas pies of their
own to make!

The Enchanted Stocking

Contents

Snowflakes and Stockings

"What a magical Christmas Eve," said Mrs. Walker, sipping her hot chocolate.

Rachel and Kirsty were sharing a large armchair in the sunroom of their cottage. Together with their parents, they had been watching the fluffy white snowflakes falling in the yard. The snow was shining icily in the moonlight, but inside it was warm and snug. Mrs. Tate had made hot chocolate with squishy marshmallows for everyone.

"Time for bed, girls," said Mr. Tate, smiling at Kirsty and Rachel as they drained their mugs. "Santa will already be on his way."

The girls felt shivers of excitement. Santa was flying through the sky on his sleigh toward them. They felt as if everything was just waiting for him to arrive—even the snow lying like a blanket over the yard outside.

"I'm sorry that we couldn't find your

stockings," said Mr. Walker. "It's very odd. I'm sure I unpacked them when we got here, but now they're nowhere to be seen."

"It doesn't matter," said Rachel, trying not to sound disappointed.

She had never had Christmas without a stocking before. She and Kirsty had both been hanging up special stockings ever since they were little.

"I bet Buttons has been chewing on them somewhere," said Mrs. Tate.

Buttons's ears drooped as he left the

room with the girls. Rachel stroked the soft fur on his head.

"Don't be upset, Buttons," she said. "I'm sure you had nothing to do with the stockings disappearing." "I agree," said Kirsty, lowering her voice in case their parents could hear her. "I think it happened because Jack Frost has stolen Natalie's magic items."

Rachel nodded. They had helped the Christmas Stocking Fairy find her magic Christmas pie, but there were still two items missing, and only a few hours of Christmas Eve left. Time was running out!

Buttons gave a curious woof and darted upstairs.

"What's the matter, Buttons?" called Rachel, taking a step after him.

Kirsty peeked through the open door of the living room. It looked very cozy and peaceful. The tree was covered in twinkling colored lights and the fire was

still dancing in the hearth, making the
whole room glow. It was perfect—except
for the bare mantelpiece.

"Somehow it doesn't seem like
Christmas Eve without stockings," she
said with a sigh.

Rachel had been about to follow
Buttons upstairs, but she turned around

and stood next to her best friend. She slipped her hand into Kirsty's and smiled at her.

"We'll make it fun—with or without our stockings," she said in a comforting voice.

Suddenly, the girls heard a tiny scratching noise.

"What was that?" exclaimed Rachel.

"It came from the fireplace," said

Kirsty, hurrying into the room.

A sprinkle of soot came down the chimney, and the fire died down.

"Oh, no," said Rachel, raising her hand to her mouth. "Do you think that a bird could be stuck in the chimney? I should go get Dad."

"Wait!" said Kirsty, grabbing her best friend's arm as she turned to leave the room. "I've got a funny feeling that it's not a bird."

The fire died down even more, and

then the girls saw a tiny pinprick of light shining in the darkness of the chimney. The light grew brighter and brighter, and then a fairy whooshed down the chimney in a whirl of silvery sparkles.

"Natalie!" said Rachel happily. "Have you found your other missing items?"

"Not yet," said Natalie, her cheeks pink. "But I think I'm very close. I followed two goblins all the way from Fairyland, and I think Jack Frost might have sent them here to hide the enchanted stocking!"

Tree
Tricks

"So the enchanted stocking might be very close by?" asked Rachel, feeling excited. "We've got a really good chance of finding it!"

Natalie fluttered up to stand on the mantelpiece so that she could look into the girls' eyes.

"It might be more difficult than you think," she said.

"Where are the goblins now?" asked Kirsty eagerly.

"That's the problem," said Natalie. "When I got here, the snow was so thick and heavy that I couldn't see a thing. I lost sight of the goblins near a tree in the yard. I don't know where they went!"

Her wings drooped a little, and the girls felt very sorry for her.

"Don't give up!" said Rachel. "Show us the tree where you last saw them. Maybe we can find a clue that will tell us where they went."

Natalie flew down from the mantelpiece and slipped under a lock of Kirsty's hair.

Then the girls tiptoed out into the hall
and pulled on their coats and boots as
quietly as they could. They slowly
opened the creaky wooden front door
and stepped out into the snowy yard.

"It's lucky that our parents are sitting
at the back of the house!" said Rachel
with a little chuckle. "They would
wonder what we were doing out in the
snow so late!"

"Which tree was it?" Kirsty asked Natalie, blinking as the flurries of snowflakes stuck to her eyelashes.

"That one over there," said Natalie, pointing at the apple tree to the left of the house.

The snow was very deep and it was hard to walk through, but at last they reached the apple tree. There were lots of marks in the snow around the tree.

"Goblin footprints!" said Rachel. "I'd recognize them anywhere."

"Me, too," said Kirsty. "Now all we have to do is follow the trail of footprints and we're sure to find the goblins."

"I don't think it's going to be so easy," said Rachel, looking puzzled. "These footprints don't go anywhere. They just go around and around the tree. It's as if the goblins have completely disappeared."

She was right. Kirsty walked all the way around the tree. She could see the footprints leading up to the tree, and going around it. But there were no footprints leading away.

"It's impossible!" she said. "Goblins can't fly."

She looked around, wondering if the goblins were watching them from the dark bushes that bordered the yard.

"Did you see anything else that might give us a clue about the goblins?" Rachel asked Natalie. The little fairy thought carefully. "The only other thing I noticed were some scratching noises as I came down the chimney," she said. "But they were coming from upstairs inside the cottage. How could the goblins have gotten inside the house without leaving footprints here?"

"I know!" said Kirsty, turning to them with shining eyes.

She had been staring thoughtfully at the tree, and suddenly she realized what must have happened.

"The goblins didn't leave any footprints because they never left the tree," she said.

"I don't understand," said Rachel. "If they never

left, then why can't we see them?"

"Because they climbed *up* the tree instead!" Kirsty exclaimed.

She pointed up to where a branch of the tree rested on a window ledge. The window was open.

"You're right—that's how they got into the cottage!" Natalie said. "Which room is that?"

Rachel and Kirsty exchanged worried glances.

"It's our bedroom!" cried Rachel. "Come on!"

Tug-of-War

The girls started to run back to the house, but it was slow going in the deep snow. It seemed like forever before they reached the front door. They flung off their snowy coats and boots, and raced upstairs to their bedroom.

The bedroom door was open, and they could hear Buttons growling from inside.

They rushed in, and then stopped in their tracks.

Two goblins were sitting on the edge of the windowsill, clutching the girls' 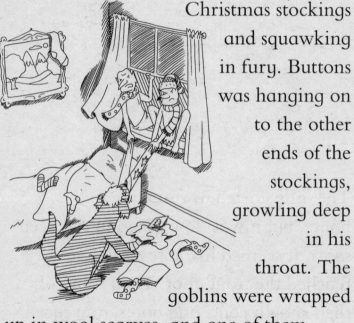 Christmas stockings and squawking in fury. Buttons was hanging on to the other ends of the stockings, growling deep in his throat. The goblins were wrapped up in wool scarves, and one of them clearly had a cold, because his nose was very red. Their bony feet were reaching out for the topmost branches of the apple tree.

"They're trying to get away!" exclaimed Rachel. "Good boy, Buttons!"

The girls raced across the room to help Buttons, but Natalie cried out in surprise and flew toward the goblins.

"That's not a hat!" she exclaimed, pointing at the goblin with the red nose. "That's my enchanted stocking!"

"That doesn't belong to you!" cried Rachel. "Give it back!"

"Leave us alone, horrible human girls!" screeched the red-nosed goblin. "A-CHOO!"

Rachel and Kirsty grabbed the ends of the stockings and pulled as hard as they could. There was a loud ripping sound.

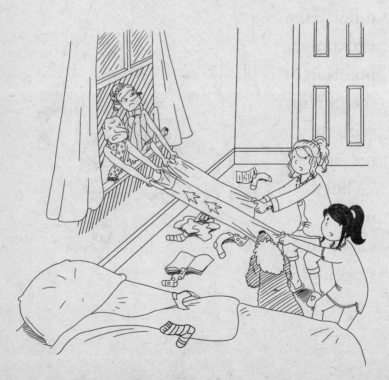

"Oooh. Three against two!" squealed the other goblin. "Not fair!"

"Pull!" yelled Kirsty.

"Hold on!" yelled the goblins.

The strange tug-of-war continued, but the goblins were struggling to stay on the windowsill. The girls and Buttons gave one last yank, and the goblins came tumbling inside the room, still clinging to the stockings. Rachel, Kirsty, and Buttons all fell backward, panting, and the goblins landed on top of them.

"Ouch!" said Kirsty, pushing the red-nosed goblin off her leg.

"Get your elbow out of my eye!" moaned the other goblin to Rachel.

Everyone sat up and tried to catch their breaths. The goblins pulled off their scarves. Natalie perched on Rachel's knee. "Why are you making so much trouble?" she asked the goblins. "You took my enchanted stocking, and now you're trying to steal Rachel's and Kirsty's stockings, too."

"That was a really mean thing to do," said Kirsty. "You shouldn't take things that don't belong to you."

"And you shouldn't mess up things that other people care about," Rachel added, holding up the ripped stockings and gazing sadly at them. "These were our favorite stockings and you've ruined them. They'll take forever to fix."

"Ruined?" exclaimed the red-nosed goblin, sniffing scornfully. "They're perfect! They're the best stockings I've ever seen. Not like this silly thing."

He pointed to the enchanted stocking, which was still on his head. Rachel and Kirsty were puzzled. "You mean, you *want* stockings that are all ripped and ruined?" asked Rachel in confusion.

The other goblin rolled his eyes at her. "Of course we do!" he said rudely. "Neat, clean stockings are for girls and fairies. Brave, handsome goblins like me want stockings like these."

"That's what you were doing here?" asked Natalie. "You were looking for stockings to hang up for Santa?"

"That's none of your business," said the
red-nosed goblin, sticking
his tongue out at her
and sneezing loudly.
"Anyway, why
shouldn't we have
stockings? Jack Frost
has one, so we should have
them, too."

The goblins started to move toward the
window, wrapping their scarves around
their necks.

"I've got an idea," Kirsty whispered to
Rachel. "I think we can get Natalie's
enchanted stocking back, but it means
that we have to give away our own
Christmas stockings!"

Stocking Swap

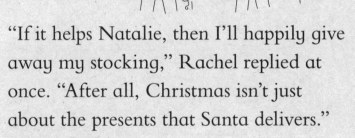

"If it helps Natalie, then I'll happily give away my stocking," Rachel replied at once. "After all, Christmas isn't just about the presents that Santa delivers."

Kirsty smiled at her.

"I thought you'd say that," she said. "If we can convince the goblins to give us the enchanted stocking in return for our stockings, we might still be able to keep Jack Frost from ruining Christmas."

The girls looked at the goblins. They were just about to climb out of the window, and were shoving each other, arguing and sounding very grumpy.

"Wait!" Kirsty called. "Please come back."

The goblins looked around in surprise.

Rachel and Kirsty held out their stockings.

"Would you like to do a swap?" asked Rachel.

"What do you mean?" asked the red-nosed goblin in a suspicious voice.

Kirsty took a deep breath. "If you give Natalie her enchanted stocking, we'll give you our ripped stockings," she said.

Natalie looked at the girls in amazement. She hadn't heard their plan, but she knew how much their stockings meant to them. She could hardly believe her ears!

The goblins took a step toward the girls.

"Really?" asked the red-nosed one,

taking the enchanted stocking off his head and holding it in his hands. "You'd really swap this horrible thing for those lovely stockings?"

"Don't believe them!" squawked the other goblin, tugging on his arm. "It's a trick! They're lying!"

"It's not a trick, and we always tell the truth," said Rachel. "Give us the enchanted stocking and I promise that you can have these stockings to keep."

The goblins went
into the corner and
whispered to each
other for a long
time. The girls
couldn't hear
anything
except an
occasional sneeze.
Natalie fluttered onto Rachel's shoulder
and they waited.

At last, the goblins turned around, and
Rachel and Kirsty held their breaths.

"We agree!" the goblins said together.

Smiling, Natalie flew over to them and
they handed her the enchanted stocking.
It returned to fairy-size as soon as she
touched it. Then Rachel and Kirsty gave
their ruined stockings to the goblins.

"Hee-hee!" squealed the red-nosed goblin in delight. "We've got two stockings for one! Those silly humans don't know how to bargain. A-CHOO!"

He ran around the room, waving his ripped stocking above his head. "Come on," said the other goblin in an impatient voice. "Let's go."

They sprang out of the window onto the branches of the apple tree and disappeared into the darkness. Rachel and Kirsty looked at each other and laughed.

"We did it!" said Kirsty. "Now there's

90

only one magic item left to find."

But Natalie didn't look as happy as they expected.

"It's wonderful that we found the enchanted stocking," she said. "But it's almost Christmas Day, and the charmed candy cane is still missing. Without it, boys and girls won't get any delicious treats this Christmas."

"We'll think of something," said Rachel kindly. "But first, let's make sure that those goblins are really leaving.

I don't want them to cause any more trouble here!"

They hurried over to the window and leaned out as far as they dared.

In the yard, they could see the two goblins climbing down the tree trunk. Their green skin gleamed in the moonlight.

"You're going too slowly," one of them complained. "Hurry up."

"Get your foot out of my eye," grumbled the other one. "I'm going as fast as I can. What's the big rush, anyway?"

"I want to try some of that stripy candy that Jack Frost has," said the first goblin. "If we're not back soon, the other goblins will have eaten it all."

"You're right," said the other goblin, speeding up. "They're all really greedy. A-CHOO!"

Natalie and the girls gazed at one another in excitement.

"Do you think they're talking about the charmed candy cane?" asked Natalie.

"Yes!" said Kirsty. "Jack Frost must be keeping it close to him—right in the heart of his Ice Castle!"

The girls exchanged a glance. They were happy to know where the candy cane was, even if it meant a trip to Jack Frost's castle.

A Sweet Surprise

The girls closed the window, and Natalie hovered beside them. Jack Frost's castle was a scary place, and there was very little time left. Could they get the charmed candy cane back before the sun rose?

"We should leave now," said Rachel, thinking out loud. "Every moment is precious."

"No," said Natalie. "You shouldn't have to help me get into Jack Frost's castle on Christmas Eve. I'll go by myself."

"No way," said Kirsty in a determined voice. "We're not letting you go there alone."

"Kirsty's right," said Rachel. "We're coming with you."

Natalie could see that she wouldn't be able to change their minds. She smiled gratefully.

"Thank you," she said. "It will be nicer to have you there with me. I'll make sure that time stands still here while you're gone, so your parents won't realize that you're not in bed."

Rachel knelt down next to Buttons and patted his shaggy head.

"You were wonderful, Buttons!" she said. "Thanks to you, the enchanted stocking is safe."

"I'd like to thank him, too," said
Natalie.

She waved her wand and cast a
magic spell.

"A loyal pet whose heart is true.
Girls whose hearts are generous, too.
Give my dog and human friends
Presents that will make amends."

There was
a puff of
sparkling
fairy dust.
When the
sparkles
cleared, a
juicy bone was
lying between Buttons's front paws.

But he wasn't the only one to be
surprised with a gift. Kirsty and Rachel
saw that two beautiful new stockings
had appeared in their hands. They were
delicately embroidered with pictures of
the girls' fairy friends.

"Thank you!"
said Rachel.

"I've never
seen such
beautiful
stockings!"
Kirsty added.

"When
Santa sees
them, he will

know that you are friends with the
fairies," said Natalie.

"Let's hang them up before we go to

the Ice Castle," said Rachel eagerly.
"Come on, Buttons!"

Rachel and Kirsty tiptoed downstairs.
Buttons ran ahead of them and flopped
down in his bed with his bone. The girls
could hear their parents talking in the
sunroom. They crept into the living
room and carefully hung their wonderful
new stockings from the mantelpiece.

"There's just one more thing to do
before we go," said Kirsty, looking at
Rachel.

"Oh, yes!" said Rachel, remembering.
"Santa and his reindeer will be hungry
when they get here."

They hurried into the kitchen and
opened the container of
mini pies that
they had made
the day
before.
Rachel
put three
pies on a
plate while
Kirsty got
some carrots from the fridge. Then they

put the treats on the mantelpiece next to their stockings.

"Ready?" asked Natalie.

Kirsty and Rachel held hands.

"Ready!" they said together.

With a swish of Natalie's wand, the girls began to shrink into fairies, surrounded by shimmering snowflakes.

Gauzy wings appeared on their backs, and they felt Natalie's magic whisking them away to Fairyland. Rachel and Kirsty couldn't wait to find Natalie's candy cane. The final part of their adventure was about to begin!

The Charmed Candy Cane

Contents

Back to Fairyland

Rachel, Kirsty, and Natalie arrived outside the Christmas Workshop in a flurry of sparkles. The three friends hurried inside, and Natalie returned the enchanted stocking to her little white box. Then she used her magic to make snug coats and boots for Kirsty and Rachel.

"Are the other Christmas Fairies here?" asked Rachel, hoping to see some of their friends again.

"No," said Natalie. "They're all at the palace with the king and queen. The night before Christmas is a very busy time for us. They're relying on me to find the last missing object."

"Not just you," said Kirsty, smiling at the little fairy. "Rachel and I are here to help you."

"Besides, there's no time to fly to the palace and ask for help," Rachel added. "It's almost midnight."

"If we can't get the charmed candy cane back before Christmas Day, no one will get any treats in their stockings this year," said Kirsty. "We have to get to the Ice Castle and find out where Jack Frost has hidden it. There's no time to lose."

They hurried out of the Christmas Workshop and fluttered up into the cold night air. After they had made their way past the trees, they reached the moonlit road to the Ice Castle.

"We have to fly like the wind," said Natalie.

With her wand she tapped first Rachel's wings, then Kirsty's, and finally her own.

"Now you will be able to fly three times as fast as before!" she said.

The girls fluttered their wings and shot forward at an incredible speed.

"It's like the best carnival ride ever!" squealed Kirsty as they raced forward.

Within a few minutes they were hovering high above the castle. There were goblins on patrol all around the battlements.

"We'll never get in while the guards are watching," said Natalie.

"Let's fly lower," said Rachel. "We might spot an unguarded way in if we get closer."

The three fairies peered around in the moonlight.

"I can't see any way in," said Natalie.

Her breath formed a cloud in the freezing night air.

"Kirsty, do you remember when we came here with Holly?" said Rachel. "We found an open trapdoor. Maybe we could get in that way again."

Kirsty looked around eagerly, but then her shoulders slumped.

"I can see the trapdoor," she said, pointing at the icy floor of the battlements. "But there are two goblin guards standing right on top of it."

It looked as if it was going to be impossible to get in. But as Rachel was staring at the goblins on top of the trapdoor, she noticed something strange.

"Do those goblins look a little odd to you?" she asked.

They flew lower. The goblins looked bigger than usual, and barely a scrap of green skin could be seen.

"They're completely bundled up
against the cold!" realized Rachel.
"Look—the one on the left has feathers
on the top of his head."

"The other one's wearing three fake
beards," added Kirsty with a giggle.

All the goblins on the battlements were the same. It was so cold that they had put on anything they could find. The girls could see blankets, turbans, sombreros, and top hats. There was even a goblin in an old-fashioned diving helmet. Each of the goblins was also wrapped in a big scarf.

"I'm still freezing," they heard one of the goblins grumble.

He was wearing a top hat that was so big that it was resting on his shoulders. His voice was very muffled.

"It's lucky we found that old box of costumes," said another from underneath a three-cornered pirate's hat.

"Jack Frost's really mean to make us work when it's so cold," said another. "I can't see a thing."

Rachel and Kirsty exchanged an excited glance.

"That's how we can get in!" said Kirsty. "They're so bundled up that they might not notice us."

"Let's try it," said Rachel eagerly. "We just have to be very, very quiet."

A Chilly Search

Soundlessly, the three friends fluttered
down to the courtyard. Rachel and Kirsty
kept their fingers crossed as they drifted
lower, hoping that the guards wouldn't
notice them. At last, they felt hard stone
under their feet. They had done it!

"Where should we start looking?" asked Natalie in a whisper.

Her voice shook a little. Rachel and Kirsty had visited Jack Frost's Ice Castle several times, but she had never been there before. It was a dank and dismal

place. Rachel gave her hand a comforting squeeze. Kirsty looked around and saw a passageway leading off from the courtyard.

"Let's start down there," she said in a soft voice.

They fluttered down the passageway.
It was lit by flickering torches, and there
were many doors on each side of it. At
the far end was a winding staircase.

"We'll have to search every room,"
said Natalie. "Jack Frost could be
keeping the charmed candy cane
anywhere."

"Let's split up," Rachel suggested.
"We'll be able to search more quickly if
we go in different directions."

The fairies checked all the rooms along the passage. They found plenty of cobwebs and lots of dust bunnies, but no charmed candy cane.

They met up at the end of the passageway.

"Any luck?" asked Natalie.

Rachel and Kirsty shook their heads.

"Let's go up this staircase," Kirsty suggested. "Perhaps he's hidden it in one of the towers."

They fluttered up the narrow, spiraling

stairs. At the top they found an empty hallway and another staircase.

"Let's keep searching," said Natalie. "But watch out for goblins!"

The girls split up again and started to search. They fluttered up staircase after staircase, through hallway after hallway, and into room after room. They saw the open costume box that the goblins had raided. They saw the drums and guitars that belonged to the Gobolicious Band. They saw the tutus and headdresses that the Goblinovski Festival Ballet dancers wore. But they didn't see a single sign of the charmed candy cane. As they came to the end of another hallway, Kirsty drew in her breath sharply.

"I can hear goblin voices!" she said urgently. "Quick—hide!"

It was so cold inside the stone walls of the castle that icicles grew from the ceilings. Rachel, Kirsty, and Natalie hovered behind three of the thickest icicles as the goblins hurried along the hallway below.

"Jack Frost has eaten all the bogmallows *again*," grumbled the smaller goblin, who was wearing a chef's hat. "He's ordered me to make another batch.

I'm tired of always making bogmallows and never getting to eat them."

"I just wish he'd let us wear warmer clothes inside," said the other. "My toes are turning into icicles!"

They disappeared down the stairs and the girls heaved sighs of relief.

"Whew, that was close," said Rachel. "Come on."

They flew up the stairs and found a single wooden door at the top. They had reached the topmost room of the highest tower.

"I hope we find my candy cane soon," said Natalie.

There were all sorts of things piled up around the room. Rachel, Natalie, and Kirsty searched through moldy plates, broken ornaments, chipped mugs, and smelly socks. Eventually, they stopped and looked at one another in disappointment.

"Nothing," said Kirsty. "That means there's only one room in the castle that we haven't checked."

"I was afraid you were going to say that," said Rachel.

"What do you mean?" asked Natalie. "Where do you think it is?"

"It must be in the Great Hall," Kirsty told her.

"That's terrific!" said Natalie. "Let's go and find it."

"If only it were that easy," said Rachel with a sigh. "You see, the Great Hall is where Jack Frost will be!"

Bogmallows and Bad Tempers

Kirsty and Rachel led the way to the Great Hall. As they flew closer, they heard many running footsteps and the squawking sound of goblin voices. The door of the Great Hall banged loudly as goblins hurried in and out. Every time the door opened, the three friends could hear Jack Frost bellowing orders at the top of his voice.

"Where are my bogmallows?"

"Get me an extra blanket!"

"Shut that door!"

The three fairies hovered close to
the ceiling.

"How are we going to get inside?"
asked Rachel.

Before her friends could reply, they saw

a worried-looking goblin
running down the
hallway toward the
Great Hall. He was
carrying a tray of
bogmallows, and the
girls realized that
he was the same
goblin they had
seen earlier. He was
still wearing his chef's hat.

The goblin's hands were full, so he used his elbow to turn the handle and open the door. He pushed it as hard as he could and it swung open.

"Quickly, let's follow him in!" said Kirsty.

As the goblin hurried through with his tray, Kirsty, Rachel, and Natalie darted inside.

Jack Frost sat on his throne surrounded by a semicircle of goblins. In the corner, a withered branch had been stuck into a Christmas tree stand, and a few ragged paper chains were looped around it. Three goblins stood around the tree, holding sheets of carol music. Their loud squawks were obviously their idea of singing, but they were making a terrible noise. Kirsty put her hands over her ears.

"I think they're all singing different carols," she groaned.

"Let's stay out of sight," said Rachel.

They fluttered up to the ceiling and perched on the chandelier so that they had a good view of the hall. At that moment, the goblin carrying the tray stepped up to the throne and bowed.

"Your bogmallows are ready," he said.

"You took your time!" snapped Jack Frost. "Give them to me."

He snatched the tray and started to gobble the bogmallows.

The goblins around him shuffled closer to the throne. They looked hungry, but Jack Frost ignored them.

As he stuffed the bogmallows into his mouth, another gaggle of goblins was trying to light a fire in the hearth. They didn't seem to know what to do, and Rachel and Kirsty watched them with interest.

"You have to rub things together," one of them said bossily. "I heard a boy scout say so."

The others started to make suggestions.

"Your hands?" said one.

"Bogmallows?" said another.

"Hats?"

"Noses?"

"Boots?"

A plump goblin started busily rubbing two old toothbrushes together.

"It's not working," he moaned.

Suddenly, Natalie noticed something. The goblins who were sitting around the throne were all drooling. She looked more closely and saw that their eyes were fixed on one of the arms of Jack Frost's throne.

"That's strange," she murmured.

At that moment, Jack Frost moved, and the folds of his cloak fell open. Tucked down the side of the throne was a long, delicious-looking striped candy with a curved handle. Natalie clutched Kirsty's arm and pointed.

"It's the charmed candy cane," she whispered. "We found it!"

A Charmed Rescue

"Look!" whispered Kirsty. "One of the goblins is trying to take the charmed candy cane."

The goblin reached out toward the sweet treat, but Jack Frost saw him and rapped the greedy hand with his wand.

"OOOW!" yowled the goblin.

"Leave it alone!" yelled Jack Frost. "You can't have that—it's mine!"

He went back to munching on the bogmallows. His face got closer and closer to the tray as he scooped them into his mouth.

"Another goblin's trying to take it now," said Rachel.

But this time, Jack Frost didn't notice.

Carefully, the goblin lifted it from the arm of the throne. He brought it slowly toward his open, drooling mouth. "Oh, no, he's going to eat it!" Natalie groaned. The goblin holding the charmed candy cane stuck out his tongue and took a long, slurpy lick.

"Yuck!" squawked
the goblin.
"Disgusting!"

He thrust the
charmed
candy cane
away from
himself, and

another goblin grabbed it and took
a taste.

"UGH!" he squealed. "Strawberries
and cream!"

"We have to stop them from tasting it,"
said Natalie in a frantic voice. "There
are so many goblins that if they all taste
it, the candy cane will be completely
eaten!"

"Maybe we could take them by

surprise and snatch it away from them,"
suggested Kirsty. "If we all pull together,
we might be strong enough."

"It's worth a try!" said Rachel.
"Let's go!"

They swooped down from the
chandelier as the charmed candy cane
was passed from goblin to goblin. Each
of them took one lick and then made a
revolted face.

"I wanted it to taste like
rotten tomatoes,"
wailed one.
"I was hoping it
would taste like
moldy pudding,"
said another
disappointedly.

As he thrust the charmed candy cane
at the next goblin, Rachel, Kirsty, and
Natalie threw
their arms
around its
curved handle.

"Pull!" cried
Rachel.

The three
friends pulled
with all their
might, and the
surprised goblin
hung on to the
end, squawking
in alarm.

"Let go!" he squealed. "Help! Fairies!"
Jack Frost turned, yelled, and grabbed

the stripy candy, shaking it as hard as he could. The three fairies were sent spinning into a corner of the Great Hall.

"This is mine!" Jack Frost bellowed, taking a big lick of the handle. "And I'M going to eat it!"

"No!" cried Natalie.

Jack Frost just laughed. "You can't stop me!"

He took a great big lick and shook his head.

"ICK! ACK! UGH!" he spat. "It's gross!"

He flung the candy away and it skidded into the corner where the fairies had landed. It came to a stop next to them, and Natalie returned it to fairy-size immediately.

"Yes!" exclaimed Rachel and Kirsty together.

Natalie raised her wand to return them to the Christmas Workshop, but then she paused and looked at Jack Frost. He had slumped down into his throne, looking very miserable.

"You might as well leave," he told them. "I should have known that my plan wouldn't work."

"What do you mean?" asked Rachel.

"Nothing ever goes right for me," Jack Frost mumbled. "I've never had a Christmas stocking, and this year is going to be just the same."

He pulled a large polka-dot handkerchief out of his pocket and blew into it noisily. The goblins stared at him in amazement. "He looks really miserable," said Kirsty.

"I almost feel sorry for him," added Natalie.

"Me, too," said Rachel. "But what are we going to do about it?"

The three friends looked at one another.

"It's Christmas. We can't leave him when he's so upset," said Kirsty firmly.

"But we can't let him have the charmed candy cane either," Rachel replied.

"It's OK," said Natalie with a little smile. "I've got an idea."

Stockings and Sleigh Bells

Natalie raised her wand and chanted a magic spell.

"*Pie, stocking, and candy cane,*
Back at home where they'll remain.
Girls and boys from east to west
Get the treats that they like best."

Santa, hear my Christmas plea,
Fill each stocking that you see.
Let this castle, cold and gray,
Be full of joy on Christmas Day."

Tiny sparkling snowflakes whooshed
out of her wand like a fountain. The

sparkles whirled
around the
Great Hall,
touching each
goblin and
finishing in the
hands of Jack Frost.
When the sparkles cleared,
every goblin was holding a horrible,
holey stocking. On Jack Frost's lap was a
large blue stocking decorated with
lightning bolts.

The goblins jumped around in excitement, and a big smile spread over Jack Frost's face.

"I hope that they all have fun opening their presents together," said Natalie. "At Christmas, one of the most important things is to have a good time with your family and friends."

."I agree," said Kirsty. "Now that we have found the charmed candy cane, I think it's time for us to go back to our families."

"And it's time for me to take the charmed candy cane back to the Christmas Workshop," said Natalie. "Thank you so much for helping me to find my magic items."

She put her arms around the girls and they hugged tightly. "We're just glad that we found them in time," Rachel replied. "Merry Christmas, Natalie!"

"Merry Christmas, both of you,"
said Natalie, her eyes shining. "I don't
need to cast a spell to know that you
are going to have a wonderful
Christmas Day."

She waved her wand and a whirl of

fairy dust
surrounded
Rachel and Kirsty,
lifting them off
their feet.
"Good-bye,
Natalie!" called
Rachel.
"Good-bye,
Jack Frost!"
When the
sparkles cleared, Rachel's and Kirsty's

warm coats were gone, and they were back in the peaceful living room of the holiday cottage. The lights were twinkling and they could hear their parents chatting in the sunroom.

Rachel looked at the clock. "It's almost midnight, just like when we left," she said. "No time has passed since we went to Fairyland."

The living room door creaked open slowly. Buttons ran in, wagging his tail. He licked their hands, delighted to see them.

"Do you think he knows that we've been on an adventure?" asked Kirsty.

"Of course he knows," said Rachel, kneeling down and patting him. "He's a very smart dog."

Suddenly, Kirsty gasped with excitement.

"Rachel, look at the mantelpiece," she whispered.

In the orange glow from the fire, they could see that the plate of pies had been replaced by a few crumbs. The stockings hanging above the fire were bulging, and there was a feeling of magic in the air. Santa had been to the cottage!

Both girls reached out to their stockings, and then they paused. They looked at each other.

"Should we wait until the morning to open them?" asked Rachel.

"That's just what I was thinking," Kirsty said. "It'll be much more Christmassy to open the presents with our parents."

They smiled at each other and then tiptoed out of the living room, with Buttons following them. As they were walking up the stairs to their bedroom, Kirsty stopped and touched Rachel's arm.

"Listen," she whispered.

In the distance they could hear the faint tinkling of sleigh bells. Santa was on his way to visit someone else. Rachel sighed happily.

"This has been one of the most Christmassy Christmas adventures we have ever had," she said. "Merry Christmas, Kirsty!"

SPECIAL EDITION

Don't miss any of Rachel and Kirsty's
other fairy adventures!
Join them as they try to help

Cheryl
the Christmas Tree Fairy!

Read on for a special sneak peek. . . .

Christmas Cabin

"Look at all the snow!" Kirsty Tate said happily.

She jumped into a powdery pile and squealed in delight.

"It's so beautiful," said her best friend, Rachel Walker. "I love it here already!"

"And you haven't even seen the inside of the cabin yet!" said her dad with a laugh. "Come on, you two. You can decorate the Christmas tree."

"Oh, yes!" exclaimed Kirsty. "Each cabin comes with its own Christmas tree, doesn't it?"

Kirsty's and Rachel's parents had been planning this Christmas trip for months. They had booked a big cabin in the country for everyone to share. It was made of brown wooden logs that glowed in the winter sunshine, and a thick layer of snow covered the roof. There was a sign on the door that read: CHRISTMAS CABIN.

The Walkers and the Tates carried their bags into the cozy cabin. A fire was crackling in a woodburning stove. Large squishy couches and armchairs filled the room, and colored Christmas lights were draped around every window. It was beautiful! There was just one problem. . . .

"Where's the tree?" asked Rachel.

Mr. and Mrs. Tate checked the kitchen, Mr. and Mrs. Walker checked the dining room, and Kirsty and Rachel checked the bedrooms. But there was no Christmas tree anywhere in the cabin.

RAINBOW magic™

There's Magic in Every Series!

The Rainbow Fairies
The Weather Fairies
The Jewel Fairies
The Pet Fairies
The Fun Day Fairies
The Petal Fairies
The Dance Fairies
The Music Fairies
The Sports Fairies
The Party Fairies
The Ocean Fairies
The Night Fairies
The Magical Animal Fairies
The Princess Fairies
The Superstar Fairies
The Fashion Fairies

Read them all!

scholastic.com
rainbowmagiconline.com

HiT entertainment

RMFAIRY8